ELEMENTARY LEVEL ENGLISH LEARNERS
BOOK OF SHORT STORIES

BY JULIET SMITH

Introduction

English Language learners often find that they progress slowly because they do not know enough vocabulary.

A quick, enjoyable way to progress is by reading stories that are not too difficult (when you know 95% of the words in the story). In this book, there are 25 interesting, short and easy-to-read stories and informative passages. Each story has a short glossary of more difficult words and an optional comprehension activity at the end for which answers are given at the back of the book.

Read, learn and enjoy!

Contents

Lost and found

Ellie was lonely and bored. There was no school for weeks as it was the summer holiday. Mum and dad had to go to work so she stayed at home alone. She watched television, then she played a game on her computer. She looked at the clock. It was only 11am. Mum and dad would not be home until 7pm. She sent a message on her mobile phone to her friends but they did not answer.

It was hot in the house. She looked out the window onto the street. There was no one in the street. Some people had gone away to the seaside for a holiday but not everyone. She left the house and walked down the street. She did not know where she was going but it was better than sitting in the hot house. She walked past some waste-ground .There used to be houses there but now it was just empty land. It was a place where people left their broken washing machines, cars and baby prams.

Something was running about on the waste-ground. It was a small animal, a puppy. She followed it. The puppy was very pretty, plump, with shiny fur and big brown eyes. It looked like a lion cub She loved it.

"Come here Lenny." She held out her hand. The puppy stopped but looked afraid. She stroked his fur. He stood still. He seemed a little afraid but let her pick him up. She carried him home. Lenny looked hungry so she gave him cold meat which she found in the fridge and some milk. He ate it all.

Mum and dad were not so happy about Lenny.

"Where does he come from?"

"He might bite the furniture!"

Mum added but did not say anything else when she saw Ellie start to cry.

"He can be my friend and keep me company when you are at work."

Mum and Dad nodded. They knew Ellie was lonely sometimes.

Lenny changed Ellie's life. They ate, played, watched TV together and Lenny even slept in his dog basket in Ellie's room.

Then suddenly one day, when she and Lenny were walking in the street, a young girl ran up to them.

"Pinky!"

Lenny ran towards the girl and was very excited.

"Oh, I've been searching for you everywhere!"

Ellie stood and watched. Lenny seemed to like the girl as much as her.

"Pinky was in the garden but went through the fence and must have got lost! I have been so sad since I lost him!"

Ellie felt sad now. Lenny was her best friend but he belonged to the girl not her.

"I'm Laura. Pinky looks so fat and happy. Thank you so much for looking after him. He was lucky to find a kind friend like you."

Ellie felt too sad to speak.

"Come with us. Let's go and have an ice-cream in the park and play with Pinky. I think us three are going to be good friends and have a lovely summer together."

Ellie did not feel so sad anymore. She had not lost her friend Pinky but found another friend Laura. This summer holiday was going to be really great!

Question

Why did Ellie not feel so sad at the end of the story?

Vocabulary

Fence (n) - metal or wooden structure put up around a garden or land

Fur (n)-animal hair

Fridge (n) or Refrigerator (n) - place where perishable foods are stored

Waste-ground (n) - Unused land

Paradise Hotel

Valerie and Barry Perkins lived in London. Valerie worked in a big hotel as a housekeeper. She enjoyed this work as she liked to make the lovely hotel rooms clean and comfortable for the guests. She worked long hours but did not mind as the hotel was a happy place and Barry, her husband who was a builder often worked late too. They worked hard like this for many years and Valerie saved money carefully for their dream until one day, Valerie received a letter.

> *Dear Mrs Perkins,*
>
> *I regret to inform you that the late Agnes Crowder has passed away.*
>
> *In her last will and testimony, she stated a wish to bequeath her main residence to you, namely Barshall House, near Minton in the county of Suffolk.*
>
> *Please, contact me at the above address at your earliest convenience.*
>
> *Yours sincerely,*
>
> *Mr Roland Swires*

Valerie made a cup of tea and sat down. She re-read the letter. Barshall House was a beautiful, big house in the countryside where she used to stay when she was a little girl. Her aunt, who had been like a second mother to Valerie, had worked for Miss Crowder as a housekeeper and had lived in the house for many years. Miss Crowder had let Valerie stay with her aunt in the big house every summer as she knew she was a sickly city child who was often ill and would get healthier in the fresh country air. Valerie had long, wonderful summers in the countryside and she used to look forward to returning there all year. It was like paradise to her. She made friends with the children in the village and they spent the warm summer days playing in the woods near the house, swimming in the river and having picnics.

While she was staying in the house she had not seen Miss Crowder very often, just at the beginning of the holiday when she arrived from London and before returning to London. Her aunt would lead her to Mrs Crowder's sitting room and she would thank her for allowing her to stay. She had not seen the house where she had had such a happy time for more than thirty years. It was just unbelievable and wonderful that now it was hers!

****

"Is this the house Val?"

Barry was standing in front of some tall metal gates looking at the front of Barshall House. The old house still looked beautiful but needed re-painting and improvement.

"It's very big. I count twelve windows just on this front part."

"Yes. I know. I told you it was big."

"And look at this garden, the lawns and the fountain!"

Val looked at the red, white and yellow rose gardens. Mrs Crowder had always had roses near the front of the house.

They went inside the house. There was a spacious kitchen and scullery, a huge dining room, sitting room, study, conservatory, drawing room, eight bedrooms as well as rooms for dressing. From the bedrooms there were views of the surrounding countryside.

"We'll have to paint it Val, before we try to sell it. Should be worth a lot of money though."

Valerie did not answer Barry at first.

"Val..?"

"Barry, we are not going to sell it."

"What? We can't live here. It's too big for us and we don't have jobs here."

"I know. But at last we can make our dream come true and make this into a wonderful hotel. People can stay and be happy here like I was when I was a child. We'll call it Paradise Hotel because here everything will be perfect so they will always want to return to this place, like I did."

"It would be very hard work Valerie. But maybe----------"

"Yes, I know but you and I enjoy working and at least now we can make our dream come true and make our own small paradise on earth."

Barry looked around. The sun was shining on the lovely garden and around the house were woods, hills and even a lake. It was like a paradise. He understood why Valerie loved it so much. He put his arm around her shoulders.

"Perhaps we could Val. Perhaps we could."

Question

Why does Val think this place is like a paradise?

Vocabulary

At your earliest convenience- as soon as possible

Conservatory (n)-a glass room attached to a house to attract the sun for plants or winter warmth

Drawing room (n)-a formal room for sitting in or entertaining guests

Housekeeper (n) - in a hotel, this person organises the room cleaning and laundry.

Paradise (n)-the perfect place where there is nothing bad

Picnic (n) - a meal eaten outside often consisting of finger foods

Will (n)-a written statement of who receives your money and goods after death

Bequeath (v) - arrange for giving of possessions after death

Wonderful (adj.) - very remarkable, especially good

The brave villagers of Eyam

Ring a ring o' roses

A pocketful of posies

A-tishoo! A-tishoo!

We all fall down

This is a well-known and very old song children still sing and dance in a ring to, today. Many people think it was first sung when the bubonic plague came to London. Why?

A **ring o' roses** refers to the round red spots which were on the plague victim's skin

A pocketful of posies are the flowers and herbs people held next to their noses in the city streets as they thought the flower smell would protect them against the plague germs.

A-tishoo! A-tishoo! is the sneezing which was a symptom of the plague.

We all fall down refers to death which often followed the red spots.

In 1665, in England, 15% of Londoners died of plague but there would have been even more if the city had not been burnt down in the Great Fire of London in 1666

Unfortunately, at this time, people in places outside London also got the plague as it spread very quickly and easily. In northern England there is the small village of Eyam. Here many of the villagers died but because of their bravery and unselfishness, no-one outside the village caught the plague. This is what happened.

In the late summer of 1665 George Viccars woke up with a headache and he felt a little sick. He lived in the village of Eyam, Derbyshire, England. He was a tailor and had received a parcel of fine cloth from London just one week before. Now one of his neighbours wanted some new trousers made from the special London cloth but he felt too ill to work. Maybe, he could make them tomorrow. However, George did not work the next day as he had a fever and red boils on his neck, under his arms and on his legs. Later these boils grew very, very big and turned black and he was in great pain inside his body. After four days George was dead.

One villager after another got ill and some died. By October many of the villagers were very scared and wanted to leave to get away from the plague. Their local priest William Mompesson in the church on Sunday asked them to be unselfish, do the right thing, think of others and not leave. Then, they would not spread the plague to other villages and towns. In the following months until November 1666 more died including Mompesson's wife.

How did this happen?

We now know that bubonic plague is spread by fleas which live on rats. There were fleas on the cloth which came from London. In those days people were dirty and did not notice if they had fleas so fleabites were common.

Every year, the villagers of Eyam still have a church ceremony to remember the good that was done by the villagers in 1665.

Question

How did George Viccars get the plague?

Put the symptoms of the plague in order of appearance:

Eg. 1. Headache and a sick feeling

Great pain

Red spots

Headache and a sick feeling

Large black spots

Fever

Vocabulary

Bubonic plague (n) - disease which spreads fast and causes many people's deaths

Ceremony (n)-formal procedure often carried out in public

Fever (n) - high body temperature

Flea (n)-small insect which lives and feeds on blood of humans and animals

Headache (n) - a pain in the head

Symptom (n)-sign of an illness or condition

Spread (v)-extend over an area

Lady Godiva

A well-known tale

"Please Leofric, please. The people are so poor and hungry because you make them pay so tax."

The Earl looked at his beautiful wife. He loved her very much but he needed money from the people of Coventry (England) so that he could govern the city well. Godiva was crying. It made him sad to see her cry but he did not want to ask for less money from the people.

"The children are dressed in rags and look so thin and................."

"All right Godiva. I will do what you want you want and ask for less tax."""

"Thank you Leo, thank you!"

Leofric really needed a lot of tax money and he wished she understood this.

Godiva took her husband's hand and kissed it with her sweet, red mouth.

"But only, only........... if you agree to ride naked through the streets of Coventry city on your favourite white horse."

"What Leofric? Are you mad? Why do you ask me to do such a terrible thing?"

"Because Godiva, my lovely, we can then see how much you really do care about the poor of this city. Of course, if you are too proud to do such a simple thing, then your love for your poor Coventry people is not very great, is it?"

Leofric turned away from her laughing. Godiva was hurt and angry.

"Our people will not suffer anymore. I will ride through the streets, as bare as a new-born baby tomorrow at 12 noon."

Leofric stopped laughing. He did not want her to do that. It would make him look like a very bad husband and he did not want people to see his wife, Lady Godiva without her clothes.

"Godiva, I................."

She walked away from him.

"Tomorrow. Noon."

Leofric's messagers shouted out this message throughout the city.

"Tomorrow at noon, stay inside your houses. Close all windows and doors. Anyone who looks out onto the street will be punished!"

The Coventry citizens did not understand at first but later they found out about Godiva's promise. How they loved their brave Lady.

****

By 12 noon the next day, the busy streets of Coventry became silent. It was if the whole city was dead as the people sat indoors will all doors and windows closed. Only the sound of the horse hooves on the road could be heard as Godiva's horse carried her through the city.

Only one person, a man called Tom was too curious to see Lady Godiva with no clothes on. He made a hole in the window shutter. The old legend is that as he looked through the hole, he became blind. From then on, he was known as the blind man "peeping Tom,' the man who nearly shamed their Lady Godiva.

Leofric also felt shamed by his brave wife's deed and asked for less tax from the people after this and the people rejoiced. The legend of Lady Godiva has been famous for nearly one thousand years.

Question

Why did the king suggest his wife, Godiva ride through the streets naked?

Vocabulary

Legend (n) - Famous and often old story that may or may not be true

Promise (n) - a fixed commitment said or written to do something

Tax (n - money people have to pay to their king or government. The money is used to run and protect a city or country.

Rejoice (v) - be glad, feel happiness

Horse Shoe Crabs

It is no surprise that these crabs which look like amphibious tanks have existed for nearly 500 million years and were here before the dinosaurs. They are found all over the world and are common along the Atlantic coast of the USA.

The biggest ones measure two feet (about 65 centimetres) from top to tail tip and can weigh as much as three kilograms. They usually live for twenty years but some go on to forty years. They live on clams, mussels, sand worms and algae so are often seen on beaches and in shallow water, up to eleven meters in depth.

Horse shoe crabs can swim on their backs although they spend most of their time on the seabed and then get onto their feet again by using their tails.

They used to be ground up and used as fertiliser and as fisherman's bait to catch eels. Another interesting fact is that they have blue blood (*hemocyanin)* and because they have something called *limulus amebocyte* in their blood, they are very useful to the medicines industry. This was discovered in 1964. *Limulus amebocyte* reacts by clotting when in contact with even small traces of *bacterial endotoxins* which can cause serious illness if they enter the human bloodstream. For this reason, blood is collected from thousands of horseshoe crabs every year. Afterwards, they are safely returned to the sea

Question:

Horseshoe crabs are useful to humans. What are the 3 ways in which they can be useful?

Vocabulary

Amphibious (adj.) - means something can live or operate on land or in water

Bacteria (n) - very small organisms that can cause disease

Bait (n) - food used by fishermen to attract fish to their hook so they can catch them.

Dinosaur (n) - creature (reptile) that lived millions of years ago

Fertiliser (n) - substance that can be used to feed plants and improve their growth and development

Grind up (v) - make a solid into small particles or into a powder

Double Act

Cherry Parker was a good actress but unfortunately, like many other actresses she often had no work. Therefore, she was very happy to see this advertisement in **Showtime** magazine one day.

> *Interesting position for those in the acting profession.*
> ***Requirements:***
> *1. 1.63m*
> *2.Female*
> *3. Blonde*
> *4.55kgs*
> *5.Pale skin with freckles on nose*
> *6. Southern English accent*
> *7.Pretty blue eyes*
> *Please apply to Box no.55*

She looked at the advertisement again. She was perfect for this role. The employer agreed.

"Goodness me! How spooky! It's like looking at myself!"

Lady Felicity Fulworth- Smith stared at her.

"You're perfect Cherry. No-one will ever notice that you are not me."

Felicity was the daughter of a well-known and very rich, important man. Her parents wanted her to go out to parties with other rich people and do things for her father like opening new schools or getting money for his charities. She hated all those things and just wanted to become an artist.

"What do you want me to do?" Cherry asked Felicity, her new employer.

"Well Cherry, I want you to do all the things my parents want me to do. For that I'll pay you thirty pounds per hour and more on public holidays. Meanwhile I will go to my secret art studio to do what I really want to do which is paint!"

****

From then on, Cherry was Felicity four times a week. Each time she would come to Felicity's apartment secretly, put on the rich girl's clothes then ask Felicity's driver to take her to Felicity's engagement. She could speak like Felicity but tried not to talk very much in case she gave false information. It was hard work but good fun being someone else until she met the handsome Teddy Horswith.

It was a sunny June afternoon and she was at a garden party.

"You don't need to stay long Cherry but daddy wanted me to go to this party to network. He thinks I should socialise more with other rich young people. Just chit -chat and remember not to accept other invitations unless you want more work of course." Felicity had advised before the party.

"Hello, Felicity isn't it?"

Cherry shook hands with a tall, handsome man with fair curly hair and blue eyes. He told her he was an actor which she knew as he was famous. She liked talking to him so much that she forgot to be Felicity and talked to Teddy about the theatre, films and the future of television. Time went fast until Teddy suddenly asked.

"Would you like to come for lunch tomorrow?"

Cherry nearly agreed but remembered Felicity's words just in time. Teddy thought she was Felicity and she was not Felicity.

"Sorry. Busy tomorrow. Must go!"

****

The job was not so much fun after this and she never saw Teddy again apart from on the stage at the theatre where he was performing or sometimes on TV. However, she thought about him often in the months that followed. She felt so sad that even Felicity noticed.

"What's the matter with you Cherry? You look like a wet, cold Sunday evening in November when there's no electricity."

"Nothing Felicity. Just a little tired. Actually, being you isn't so easy."

"I know Cherry. Look at these, I keep getting love letters from some silly boy, Timmy or Tommy Horsley or something like that, I don't even remember meeting him. It's such a bore!"

Cherry looked at the signature on the letter.

Yours truly,

Teddy Horswith

She checked the sender's address.

"Don't worry Felicity. These are meant for me! Sorry Felicity. No more of you. I think I'm just going to be Cherry from now on."

****

Teddy was really pleased to see her and confused when she asked him to call her Cherry not Felicity. Eventually he understood and thought that she must be a very good actress to be able to impersonate someone for such a long time. She now has Teddy as her boyfriend and a part in a play at a famous London theatre.

Unfortunately for her, Felicity now has to go to parties herself and no-one believes her when she tells them that she used to pay the well-known actress Cherry Parker to do this for her.

Question

What adjectives would you use to describe Felicity?

Vocabulary

A **double act** normally refers to a performance on stage or television which includes two people. Here it refers to the fact that Cherry looked like Felicity (her double) and pretended she was her in real life

Engagement(n)	A social event that you have agreed and/or planned to attend previously
Signature(n)	Write your name
Perfect(adj)	100% good
Network(v)	Mix with other people for a purpose
Impersonate(v)	Pretend you are somebody else not yourself
Chit chat(v)	Talk about everyday matters
Socialise(v)	Meet and talk with others for pleasure or business

The strange story of Madeleine Smith

This story is famous in Britain and there was even a film made about Madeleine Smith in 1950.

In 1855, Madeleine Smith was the pretty daughter of a well-known, rich architect in Glasgow, Scotland. In those days, rich girls did not work or have much freedom but had to prepare themselves for marriage and husbands that their parents chose for them.

Madeleine was different and more adventurous than other rich girls at that time. One of her next-door neighbours introduced her to a gardener called Emile L'Angelier. He was a French speaker. The two young people fell in love. They often sent love letters to one another and met secretly. Madeleine knew that her parents would never let her marry Emile who asked her to marry him, so she refused.

Even worse, her parents found a rich husband for Madeleine called William Minchon. She became very afraid that William and her parents would find out about her secret boyfriend Emile so she begged him to burn her love letters. He got angry and refused. He wanted her to marry him. He said that he would show her parents the letters if she did not marry him.

Over the next few weeks, Emile became ill and his health got worse and worse. Madeleine was seen buying arsenic, a well-known poison from a chemist. Eventually Emile had such bad stomach pains that his landlady called a doctor who gave him morphine for the pain. Emile was dead by the next day. Doctors later found a large amount of arsenic in his stomach.

Madeleine was arrested and her trial became famous all over the world. In the end, Madeleine went free as the judge gave the first **'not proven'** verdict in Scottish legal history. **Not proven** does not mean that Madeleine was thought of as innocent but that there was not enough evidence to show she had killed Emile.

For example, Emile started to get ill before Madeleine bought the poison, arsenic. Madeleine said she bought the arsenic to put on her skin to whiten it. She mixed it with water to do this. This was a well-known skin whitener at the time. Some people said that Emile wanted to die but also wanted to make Madeleine suffer (die) so made it look like poisoning to make everyone think that she was a murderer.

No-one will ever know what really happened as Madeleine disappeared and it is not clear when or even where Madeleine died so the secret died with her.

Question

Madeleine Smith's court case is famous in Scottish legal history, why?

Vocabulary

Architect (n) - a designer and planner of buildings

Arsenic (n)-poison often used in weed-killing chemicals

Morphine (n) - pain relieving drug made from opium

Legal (adj.) - of the law

Arrest (v)-lawfully take a suspect

True Love

Annette's beautiful face looked so sad that morning as he sat down next to her in the lecture theatre. Rob smiled but did not know what to say so he waited until the professor had finished speaking.

"What's the matter Annette?"

She did not answer at first. It made him feel miserable as well to see her like that.

"Vincent is leaving town as he has been offered a very good job in London and I don't know if I will see him again if he leaves. I love him, Rob. What shall I do?"

Rob really did not like it when Annette said she loved Vincent but he wanted to help her. He was her old and good friend. He hated to see her unhappy and would do anything to make her smile again.

"Well, ask him not to go."

Annette looked angry.

"I can't do that. The London job is a wonderful opportunity for Vincent. It would be selfish and wrong to do that."

He looked at his sweet Annette who was now crying. There was another thing she could do which would make him even unhappier as he would miss her so terribly.

"Well you could go with him to London."

"Yes Rob. I've thought of that but he never suggested that to me. Do you think he doesn't want me to go with him?"

Annette always thought he had the answers to all her questions. He wished he had.

"I don't know Annette. He probably wants you to go to London but thinks you should finish your university degree. He wants the best for you too, you know."

"Thanks Rob. You're such a good friend."

She kissed him on the cheek.

"You always make me feel better. You are so kind. Sorry to cry but I do love Vincent so much. I don't know how I can carry on without him."

Rob held her hand. He felt the same about Annette but he was thankful that at least they were friends. It was better than nothing.

"Leave it to me Annette. It will be ok. You'll see."

She looked puzzled.

****

He did not like Annette's boyfriend Vincent. He was unpleasant and arrogant and he did not treasure Annette's love.

"I don't think you should go Vincent. Annette loves you. You'll regret it."

Vincent drew on his cigarette.

"I know she loves me but London's a big place, I'm young and there are plenty more fish in the sea. Do you see what I mean?"

Rob shook his head.

"Annette's a special girl."

"For you maybe but it's ok, I know how to make Annette happy again."

"What do you mean Vincent?"

"You'll see."

****

He did not see Annette for a few days. She seemed to be avoiding him then after class one day she came to him.

"I've been such a silly, blind fool Rob. Vince told me you went to see him for me.'

"Yes. I wanted to help you. We're friends aren't we?"

"Yes. You are a very good friend to me and I'd like to be a better friend to you."

Rob smiled. Annette was not sad anymore.

"You told Vincent I was special."

Rob blushed. He disliked Vincent even more. Now Annette would avoid him. How embarrassed he felt!

"I think you are special too Rob and I've been a silly fool."

He felt confused.

Annette took his hand and from that moment Rob knew that Vincent was not important to her anymore.

Question

Why did Annette say that she had been a fool?

Learning how to recognise parts of speech is important in learning English.

For example: beauty (noun), beautiful (adjective), to beautify (verb), beautifully (adverb)

Fill in the missing adjectives and nouns. Words from the text have been used. * has been done for you

Noun	Adjective
	Silly
Misery	
	Angry
*Happiness	Happy
	Arrogant
Foolishness	
	Embarrassed
Blindness	

A taste of his own medicine

Tom and his friend Jim went to visit his Auntie Agnes. She was pleased and surprised to see Tom as she had not seen him for a few years. Her house looked different inside to him.

"Where are all your beautiful ornaments and china tea sets Auntie? You used to have them all over the house. "

The old lady looked sad.

"I had to sell them Tom. The house needed a new roof and I had no money to pay for it. I asked the local antique dealer Fothergill to come and buy the things he wanted. He bought nearly everything apart from this silly china dog."

"How much did he pay you?"

"Oh, about a hundred pounds I think."

"A hundred pounds! But all your treasures were worth a lot more than that. Thousands in fact! You had all that fine china that had belonged to your great grandmother."

Auntie Agnes shrugged and tears came to her eyes.

"Never mind, Auntie. At least you have fewer things to polish and clean now which is good."

"That is true Tom. I was getting a little tired of looking after all those things."

Tom suddenly had an idea.

"Auntie? May I borrow this china dog?"

"Tom. Please, please keep the dog. I don't need it. If you like it, have it."

****

Tom and Jim drove home after the visit. Tom was angry.

"That antique dealer cheated my auntie badly. I don't like people who cheat especially old people like my aunt. I think he 'deserves a taste of his own medicine.'

"What do you mean Tom?"

"Well what sort of low-life takes an old lady's treasures for so little money? I am going to cheat him now and get some of his money for my aunt. Will you help?"

Jim laughed.

"How?"

"Well, I'll tell you my plan I want to ----------------"

****

The next afternoon Jim put on a good tweed jacket and slipped a leaflet in his pocket. He parked near Fothergill's and went into the antique shop. It was full of old furniture, vases and china. Some of it was ugly and just looked like old junk. Fothergill was more of a junk than antique dealer.

"Can I help you?"

It was Fothergill the shop owner. He was tall, thin and looked bad-tempered.

"Yes possibly. I have a client who collects these rare china cats. There were only very few made in the nineteenth century. He has ten of them. He wants the other five. He is willing to pay a lot if one can be found."

Jim gave Fothergill the leaflet which showed a picture of the china cat and the small stamp at the bottom of it.

"It must have this stamp on it'."

Fothergill read the leaflet and looked at the stamp. He looked red and excited.

"How much would your client pay for one?"

"Oh, two, maybe three thousand pounds! Anyway, just give me a call if you find one. I'll pay a good price for it."

"Yes certainly. I'll keep a look out."

****

Tom was not very surprised to get a telephone call from Aunt Agatha two days later.

"Mr Fothergill, that man from the antiques shop, is asking about the china dog I gave you Tom. He says he wants to buy it."

"Tell Mr Fothergill auntie that I'll bring it to his shop tomorrow."

Tom waited two days before he visited the shop. He wanted Fothergill to get impatient.

"Ah, you have the cat. Splendid! May I see it?"

Fothergill looked at the bottom of the ornament to see the sign.

"Mm, this is quite nice I'll give you a hundred pounds for it. OK?"

Tom stroked his chin.

"Sorry Mr Fothergill. I've heard that these are valuable and auntie especially likes this cat. That's why I asked my aunt if I could borrow if for valuation."

"Ok, one hundred and twenty pounds."

Tom began to wrap up the ornament again as if he was going to leave the shop.

"We both know this is valuable. Sorry Mr Fothergill I'd like a lot more money for it than that."

Fothergill looked a bit angry but smiled.

"All right Tom. My last offer is seven hundred pounds."

"Twelve hundred, please."

Fothergill breathed deeply.

"All right. Twelve, but not a penny more.

****

Auntie Agatha was very surprised when Tom gave her twelve hundred pounds.

"Why Tom?"

Mr Fothergill gave me that money for the cat.

"But the cat was a pretty but cheap thing my mother bought years ago at the seaside."

"I know aunt. But Fothergill thinks it's worth two or three thousand pounds."

The old lady looked confused.

"You don't need to know auntie."

****

Fothergill spent a long time ringing the number on the leaflet Jim had given him. Then he sat back and smiled. The man in the tweed jacket seemed desperate to find one of these awful cat ornaments. He would come back and then he could sell the cat to him for three thousand pounds and make a lot of money. Why worry? "Good things come to those who wait' was a saying he often heard. He just needed to be patient and wait.

Question

There is an expression, 'two wrongs don't make a right." What are the two wrongs done in this story?

Vocabulary

A taste of his own medicine- be treated in the same way you have treated another

Valuation (n)-a calculation of how valuable something is

Confused (adj.)-not sure or not understanding

Patient (adj.) - wait peacefully

Cheat (v)-to mislead someone for your own interests

Leaflet (n) - piece of paper promoting or informing about something or someone

Low life (n)-an unscrupulous person (colloquial usage)

Treasure (n) - a person or thing of high value

Hallowe'en

You will probably know about this festival which takes place on the 31st October every year. Children dress up as witches, wizards, ghosts and frightening monsters. When darkness comes, in groups or alone, they visit their neighbours' houses. They knock on the doors and when the neighbour opens the door, they shout 'trick or treat.' In other words, their message means that the householder must give them a treat or be punished with a trick.

Treats usually include sweets, cookies or maybe apples, particularly toffee apples. Tricks are not usually carried out by disappointed witches and monsters but in some places, they throw eggs or flour at people's houses to punish them for their lack of generosity and even paint but this is very rare as ' trick and treating' is meant to be fun and not a time to be nasty. Householders who are 'tricked' may get angry too and spoil the evening.

Have you ever wondered why American, British and children all over the world do this? You may be surprised to learn that this started as a festival more than two thousand years ago. For the Celts of the Britain celebrated Sannhain, the end of summer and the beginning of winter, their new year.

They believed that at Sannhain, the barrier between the world of the dead and the world of the living weakened so that the dead could visit the living. Therefore, on this day, they welcomed their dead ancestors to their homes and lit the way with lanterns. To frighten away evil spirits, they dressed themselves up in scary costumes.

When the Celts became Christian, they adapted their new religious celebrations to fit in with their old pagan or Celtic beliefs so they chose the 1st November as All Saints Day when the dead saints of the Church and dead family members are remembered. This meant that the old Celtic New Year, Sannhain became known as Hallowe'en which means the evening (e' en) before the holy ones (hallowed).

Question

1. Why did the Celts have many lanterns at Hallowe'en?

Vocabulary

Barrier (n)-Fence or obstacle

Generosity (n)-act of giving freely

Evil spirits (n) - very bad forces /beings

Disappointed (adj.)- do not get what you want

Words that wound

A woman had a daughter who was beautiful, intelligent and usually a good girl but she had one terrible flaw in her character. She sometimes got angry and would shout and say hurtful things to servants, friends and even people in her own family.

One day, after she had shouted at her younger sister, she sat down and cried.

"Why am I so bad-tempered? I say unkind things to the people I love. I wish I could stop getting annoyed."

Her mother heard this and left the room but returned holding a hammer and some nails.

"Can you see what I have here?"

"Of course I can. Do you think I'm stupid? You are holding a hammer and some nails."

"That's right and do you see this beautiful wooden chair here?"

"Yes. I'm not blind. You know it's the chair I love. The wood is so perfectly smooth and shiny."

"Well, every time you get angry in the next week, I want you to take a nail and hammer it into the chair."

The girl stood up.

"You cannot possibly be serious. I love that chair so why should I damage it?"

"Do as I say. You will understand later."

The girl wanted to disobey her mother but also wanted to stop getting angry. Therefore, she did what was asked and by the end of the week, the once lovely chair looked very ugly with many nails stuck in it.

"The chair looks awful. Do I have to continue?"

The mother nodded.

After three more weeks there were even more nails in the chair but the girl found she was losing her temper less and less.

Her mother noticed this and smiled.

"Look how ugly the chair is now! But you can make it look better. If you can pass a whole day without losing your temper, you can take out one nail."

The daughter felt happy. She was learning to control her anger and indeed after a few weeks she had pulled out all the nails she had hammered in earlier. The chair looked much better without the nails but not as beautiful as before. This made her sad. Her mother came to her.

"Do you see how damaged the chair looks even without the nails?"

The girl nodded.

"Each hole you see in the wood is just like the wound you leave in the heart of the person you hurt when you get angry. If like removing the nail from the chair, you say sorry to the wounded one, the damage remains, just like the hole in the chair."

The girl understood and never lost her temper again.

Questions

1. Do you believe this is a good way to teach someone to behave well and not lose their temper?

2. Reflect on a fault in your character (or someone you know). How could you or this person be taught to remedy this fault?

Vocabulary

Flaw (n)-weakness or mistake

Nail (n) - metal piece used in carpentry to attach things

Temper (n) - angry mood

Wound (n) - deep cut done to a human or animal

Damage (v - harm or injury

Disobey (v - not do as asked

Notice (v) - see, come to one's attention

Ugly (adj.) - very unattractive looking

Baby Sherman

"Ben. Stop playing on the computer and come here! You must go to Sherry's house and look after the baby. She's got toothache and I can't look after baby Sherman as I've got to go to work now. OK?"

It was not okay. Ben wanted to play 'Enemy Invader' on his computer and baby Sherman was the most boring person in the world although maybe his sister Sherry was a very close second.

"Oh no, not Sherman, mum. All he does is drink milk, scream and drop his toys on the floor. He's horrible."

"Exactly. Now go to your sister Sherry's house now. The poor girl is in great pain and must go to the dentist immediately."

****

Baby Sherman was screaming when he arrived at Sherry's house. She gave the baby to him and left. Ben looked at the baby's red face and closed his eyes as the noise from the baby's mouth was very loud.

"Shut up Sherman."

Like magic, he stopped screaming and stared at Ben with round blue eyes. Then he began to laugh. For a minute, Ben almost liked Sherman.

"Shall we play cars Sherman?"

Ben sat on the carpet and began to get toy cars out of a box. Ben helped but when he looked around the baby was not there.

"Oh no! Sherman!"

He had forgotten that Sherman could crawl now. He looked everywhere. Sherry would be very angry if he lost her baby. She had only had him for eight months and he was the centre of her life. He heard a laugh. He looked through the kitchen window. Sherman was in the garden and it was raining too. The very dirty and muddy baby was putting soil from the garden into his mouth.

"Have you been eating soil silly baby?"

Sherry would be furious. And Sherman might get ill. He took Sherman to the bathroom and put water in the bath. He put his elbow in the water to check it was not too hot. Sherry always did that. He put the baby's dirty clothes in the washing basket and hoped Sherry would not notice they were muddy.

Sherman seemed to like his bath. Ben threw a little water at him. This made the little boy laugh and he copied Ben and shook his wet hand in Ben's face. Ben made an angry face and Sherman laughed even more. They played like this for a long time until Ben noticed that the bathroom carpet was wet. Now Sherry would know the baby had had a bath.

He dressed the baby then tried to dry the bathroom floor and watch Sherman at the same time. He looked round to see Sherman playing with his jacket.

"Oh no! Leave it alone Sherman!"

But the baby was holding something. It was a twenty pound note.

"Heh! Clever baby!"

He thought he had lost the money a week before but somehow Sherman had found it. It had probably slipped into the lining of his jack. It was lucky as he had no money at all and it was mum's birthday soon.

He was thirsty so Sherman must be too. He found some fruit juice in the fridge and gave some to Sherman in his baby cup and had some himself. They both had a biscuit too although the baby only sucked on his as he had no teeth.

"Well this is a nice peaceful scene. You must be good at looking after babies Ben."

Sherry was back and she seemed happier.

"Hope it wasn't too boring for you.'

Ben looked at his watch. It was 5pm. He had been with Sherman for three and a half hours.

"No. the time went fast. It wasn't boring at all.'

He looked at Sherman who began to laugh again.

"Anytime you need a babysitter, Sherry, I'll do it."

"Thanks Uncle Ben.'

"Uncle?'

Of course he was Sherman's uncle. Suddenly he felt old and proud and knew he would visit Sherman again soon.

Question

Why did Ben like looking after Sherman? Give three reasons.

Vocabulary

Babysitter (n)-someone who looks after babies

Elbow (n) - outer part of joint in the middle of a person's arm

Muddy (adj) - lots of mud/ dirt from outside soil

Copy (v) - do the same as someone else

Notice (v) - see and take note

Shake (v)-move forcefully or quickly backwards and forwards or up and down

Tell Tale

When he was young, Terry Smith did a very bad thing. He robbed a small jewellery shop and when the owner tried to stop him, he hit the older man on the head with a jewellery case. The old man fell to the floor and never moved again. He was horrified and ran away. Of course, the police caught him, he was charged with manslaughter and went to prison for fifteen years. He was still young, just 35 when he left prison

He moved to another part of the country, got a job, married and had children. He was happy for a long time until one day as he was walking past old Mrs Crawford's house, number 21, she waved from her doorway and called to him.

He went up to her door. She was quite old, fat and usually seemed short of breath. He thought she probably wanted him to help her do a household job like change a light bulb or catch a mouse. He liked to help the neighbours and was known for it. He was a changed person and only wanted to do good now. In fact he had even changed his name. He hoped he could help her.

However, Crawford did not want his help- just his money.

"I know all about you Terry. Sorry, did I say Terry? I meant to say Frank but don't worry, it is easy to keep me quiet."

"What do you want Mrs Crawford?"

"I'm glad we understand each other. Five hundred. Just give me a Christmas box in a nice card every year and believe me, I can be very forgetful. Do you understand?"

He did understand and gave her Christmas gift in a card every year for seven years. Then one year, she suddenly asked for more money- a lot more.

"I can't give you so much. Sorry Mrs C., I just don't have the money. My job is not very well-paid."

"Oh come on! I'm sure you can Frank. You will find a way. See you in December."

He was not rich. What could he do? He was afraid.

Mrs Crawford might ask for more and more money and then tell everyone about him if he did not pay. He had a new life now which included a nice family and kind friends. They would not like him anymore if they knew about his past.

He got an idea. A terrible idea but it was the only end to his problem.

He would visit the old woman as usual before Christmas. She usually asked him in so she could count the money. He would knock her out then take her to the top of her stairs and throw her down so it would look as if she had fallen down the stairs. It was the only way. As long as nobody saw him enter her house, he would be safe for ever.

He waited until a week before Christmas. It was 5pm and already dark as he knocked on the old woman's door. He knocked once, twice then many times. He thought she must be away so he went home.

He now felt impatient to see her so that he could do what he had to do. The following afternoon, and on the following days there was still no answer. After that he waited until Christmas Eve. Surely, she would be home by then. He knocked on the door. He now felt worried. She must be there. He shone his torchlight through the letterbox and saw Mrs Crawford lying completely still on the floor at the bottom of the stairs. He called for an ambulance. He really wanted to help now. It was the right thing to do.

"I came to see her to give her a Christmas card. I always do that." he explained to the ambulance-man

"She's lucky to have such a kind neighbour," he said as he re-checked Mrs Crawford's pulse and heart.

"Sorry sir. This lady's been dead for days. Was she your friend? I guess she had a nasty fall down those stairs. "

The other neighbours said that Terry was a good man and a caring neighbour as Mrs Crawford was known to be a difficult (even unpleasant!) person and how kind it was of him to take her a Christmas card every year!

Frank or Terry as he was now known just smiled and after a while forgot all about the real reason for his visit to the old lady's house that dark afternoon.

Question

Name one way in which Frank was lucky and one way in which he was unlucky.

Vocabulary

A Christmas box- money given to tradesmen at Christmas time as a show of appreciation

Manslaughter-An unlawful killing without intention

Neighbour (n)-one who lives nearby

Tell-tale- someone who tells someone in authority or other people about your mistake or misdeed

Completely (adv.)-100%

Horrified (adj.)-filled with horror

Impatient (adj.) - get angry when waiting

Unpleasant (adj.) - not nice

One good turn deserves another

Bill Griffith had no job again and his wife was unhappy. Soon they would have their third child. To make matters worse, it was winter and freezing cold.

"We have no money for new coats for the children and I can't get more work now as I will have the baby soon."

Bill looked sadly into his teacup.

"I'm very sorry Myra but you know there is not much building work in the winter and Mr Jackson probably doesn't want me to drive the lorry to Holland this weekend."

"I don't really want you to be far away in Europe this weekend. You have spent so many weekends away driving Jackson's lorry. It is dangerous in the winter."

It was true that Bill spent many weekends away from home delivering goods to Europe. Mr Jackson, the haulier gave him the work. It was good money but tiring. He had done this for many years. Things were bad for his family at the moment but hopefully they would get better.

The doorbell rang.

"Maybe it is Peter or David returning the money you lent to them. You are crazy lending money when you have no job and have a family to feed. I know they always ask you because you're kind and helpful. But you should remember that 'charity starts in the home' Bill."

"Now, now, don't get angry Myra. Think of the baby."

When he reached the door, there was no-one there but a letter lay on the floor. Something dropped out of the envelope as he pulled the letter out. It was a cheque for £200,000.

Myra stared at the cheque and held it up to the light.

It's a real cheque Bill with your name on it. It must be a mistake or a bad joke."

The letter was from a lawyer, a D. Willis, the same person who had signed the cheque.

'I am acting on behalf of a client who wishes you to receive this gift of money. He declines to be named but has one message only.

A small price to pay.

From your old mate who scarpered.'

Yours sincerely,

Mr D Willis

(Willis and Crabtree Solicitors)

"I don't understand Bill. Who sent this money to us?"

"I have no idea Myra.'

"We could ask the lawyer, Mr Willis."

"The lawyer says in the letter that he can't tell us who gave the money."

"Bill. I can hardly believe it. It's so much money. What shall we tell people? They'll think we stole it."

"Don't tell them anything."

The telephone rang. It was Mr Jackson from the haulage company.

"Bill. Got a load here from Harland Company Limited. Needs to be in Rotterdam by Monday. Could you do us a favour and take it over tonight? It's a bit of an emergency."

"No problem Mr J. I'll be there at 6."

"Why did you agree to that? You don't need to do these jobs now."

"Myra. This letter and cheque is probably a mistake or joke so we should just carry on as usual until we are certain."

Myra was quiet for a minute.

"You're probably right. I'll try to pay the cheque in tomorrow and see if the bank accepts it or should I telephone the solicitor?"

"Do both."

****

Bill enjoyed the drive to Holland despite the snow and icy conditions. It gave him time to think about the letter and cheque. Who would play a trick on him like this and why? And if it was real, who was the benefactor?

He only slept a few hours before starting the journey home. He did not want to leave Myra alone for too long in case the baby came early. He drove off the car ferry at Harwich then took the road north. There was noise in the back of the truck so he stopped to check. It was a loose lock.

It was then he remembered another cold dark night a long, long time ago, just outside Harwich. He had heard a bump and a cry as he swerved sharply. He had stopped the truck just like now. He had opened the back of the truck and in a dark corner he had found a man half-conscious and blue with the cold.

The man had been terrified.

"Pleez, pleez Mister. I go. OK?"

Bill had driven the man to a quiet country area. He gave him some hot tea from his vacuum flask and the sandwiches and cake Myra gave him for his trips. The man was very hungry. Slowly his blue skin became pink again. Bill did not know what to do. He could go to prison for helping this man who was an illegal immigrant. He wished he had never seen this man. Mr Jackson had even told him to be careful about this. On the other hand, Bill felt very sorry for the thin, very scared man. If he had not heard him, he may never even have known about this man. He gave him a ten pound note and then pointed to himself.

"Me! Never see you. OK? Now scarper, me old mate."

Bill could remember watching the man run and disappear into the trees as he drove away. It was a secret and it was going to stay a secret forever.

Myra was full of news on his return. I spoke to the lawyer at his office. It all seems all right but he wouldn't tell me the name of the person who gave you the money. The bank accepted his cheque and if it clears we'll be £200,000 richer. But who is the donor? Have you worked it out yet?

Bill shook his head and carefully did not look at his wife when he answered.

"You know my memory is terrible Myra but perhaps I will remember one day."

Myra knew her Bill was kind but not very clever so she was sure that the generous donor was someone he had helped in the past. Bill was always doing things like that.

Question

1. Myra said 'charity starts at home." What did she mean?

2. Myra said that Bill was kind. Find two examples of Bill's kindness.

Vocabulary

Point (v) - indicate with finger

Scarper (v) - Slang. Go away fast

Swerve (v) - Sudden change of direction after driving straight

Benefactor (n) - Someone who gives money or services to another person.

Donor (n) - a giver of something (for example, money or blood)

Cheque (n) - payment in place of cash. Issued by bank.

Mate (n) - friend (slang)

Solicitor (n) - Lawyer who does less work in court

Stolen Good

Chas looked at the beautiful rosewood box. It was patterned and decorated with precious stones. Inside there were some pearl necklaces, ruby rings, diamond bracelets. Scoffer, a man he knew would buy this jewellery and then he would have lots of money to spend on Christmas presents for Sheila and Trevor.

When he had broken into the house the night before, he just wanted money, watches, mobile phones and things which he could sell very quickly. He had no job and it was getting difficult for himself and his family, He did not know why he took the box as it was heavy but he saw it in the old man's bedroom and liked it. Now he was glad that he had stolen it as it had expensive jewels in it.

"You look happy Chas. Why were you so late coming home last night?"

"Met some old friends and had some drinks Sheel."

His wife smiled. She always believed his stories and liked him to enjoy himself. He could not tell her that he had gone into a stranger's house last night and stolen from him even if he had done it for the family not just himself. He left Sheila in the kitchen and went into the garden to the shed. Sheila and Trevor, his son never went in his shed. They knew it was his special place where he made things but they did not know he hid stolen things there.

He took the jewellery out of the box and put it in a backpack. He found an old cloth to wrap around the box. He did not want it to get scratched in his bag. It was then he stupidly dropped it onto the shed floor. He swore as now the box would be scratched or damaged. He picked up the box and dusted it as the shed floor was dirty. His hands were dirty. A piece of wood inside the box was now loose. He felt excited as he could see paper. Maybe it was money. It was not. It was an old letter. He wanted to throw the letter away at first but he was curious about it. Why was it hidden?

On the envelope, there was an address:

To be delivered on my death

Mr Henry Platter,
12, Lervet View,
Kellenvale,
Hertfordshire,
HE12 UYT

He felt bad opening a private letter but he wanted to see if there was money inside.

Dear Henry,

When you read this, I will not be alive but I want you to know that it is the greatest sadness to me that our friendship ended. I am sincerely sorry for the wrong I did you and I hope you can find it in your heart to forgive me.

I.........................

Yours truly,

Sam.

Chas felt sad. Henry Platter used to be the old man's friend. He was curious about what the old man had done to Henry. May be he could help the old man since he had helped him get richer for Christmas. He would feel better then about stealing from him.

He went to number 12, Lervet View and posted the letter that night at 3am to make sure he was unseen. He wondered if Sam and Henry would become friends again and hoped they did. He, Sheila and Trevor had a lovely Christmas but just before New Year, Chas had a very bad shock.

The door bell rang. A policeman stood there and asked him to go to the police station for questioning. They knew about the burglary because he had stupidly left dusty fingerprints all over the letter he had taken to Lervet View. His act of kindness, it seems, had led to his arrest and certainly a prison sentence.

He sat in the police station cell and wondered what to say to Sheila and Trevor. The police would probably not let him free now. Two policemen came to his cell and unlocked it.

"You can go."

"Go? Why?"

"Two old men just came to the station and the one who had brought the charges said it was all a mistake for some reason."

"What?"

The policeman shrugged.

"Your lucky day Chas. He says he is old and confused and forgot that he gave you the jewellery box."

Chas agreed that it was his lucky day and he was even happier now that he knew he had brought happiness to the old man he had robbed.

Question

Why did Chas burgle the house?

What was his 'act of kindness'?

Vocabulary

Confused (adj.)-not understand or remember fully

Backpack (n)-type of bag carried on the back

Cell (n) - room prisoners live in,

Charge (n) police claim you are guilty of a crime

Jewellery (n) - things made for decoration in gold, silver, gems etc.

Rosewood (n) - a type of fragrant close-grained wood used for furniture etc

Shed (n - small often wooden hut used for gardening and other hobbies

Scratch (v) - make a mark on the surface of something

Shrug (v) - to raise shoulders to convey uncertainty

Parents' Evening

Mrs Oliver felt strange in her old school that evening. She was there to see her daughter Mel's teacher, Ms Brown about Mel's schoolwork. She did not want to see Ms Brown as she knew Mel was not a clever school pupil. She found Mel's classroom. She had to wait outside the classroom while Ms Brown talked to some other parents before it was her turn.

She stood in the corridor and remembered her old friends as children wearing the same school uniform that Mel wore. She even thought she heard the tip tap of Ms Cornell's heels along the corridor. Dear Ms Cornell- how she had loved old Corny with her shiny silver bell which she used to ding to silence them and all her 'corny' sayings.

"You're all such treasures children, every one of you and I am only the old miner here to dig out your precious gifts and smooth the rough edges away.'

She had wagged her finger as she said this.

"Every human being is unique and as valuable as the next person. Remember that children."

Their young chests had swelled with pride.

"Don't hide your light under a bushel children. Shine out to make our beautiful world an even lovelier place."

Nowadays people would laugh at her but she inspired many pupils.

"Mrs Oliver."

It was her turn to see the teacher. Mel's teacher was very nice and read out Mel's marks to her. She looked sad.

"I'm afraid she's only a level E maybe D. The average is a C obviously. Maybe she could be a C if she had a tutor?"

Ms Brown seemed sorry about Mel. Mrs Oliver kept thinking about Ms Cornell whilst Ms Brown talked about this grade and that grade.

"We all have a talent." Ms Cornell used to say when she was at school.

 Don't bury it in the ground to rust and rot. Polish it children so that we can all enjoy its bright magnificence!"

"Mel has a talent for drawing you know.'

She said suddenly. Ms Brown frowned.

"That maybe true but that doesn't help her reading age which is....."

A bell rang.

"Miss Cornell?"

"Miss Cornell? No Mrs Oliver. Sorry it's time for the next parent."

****

Mel was still drawing when Mrs Oliver reached home.

"What did Ms B say?"

Mrs Oliver looked at Mel's drawing. It was very good.

"You have a gift for drawing Mel. Keep on practising and you will become very skilled and bring pleasure to the world."

Mel gave a big smile. Mum seemed happy so she was happy too.

Match the words with their definitions

Word from text	Definition
Talent(n)	On object or collection of special, valuable objects
Gift(n)	Often long and thin. An area leading to rooms
Treasure(n)	Only one thing or person like this
Precious(adj.)	A natural ability for something
Corridor(n)	Rare and difficult or impossible to replace
Unique(adj.)	A natural ability for something

Vocation

"What are you doing today Anna?"

"Not sure, mum. Maybe I'll go shopping with Nina or go to the beach."

"Anna, you have left school now but you have no job or even any idea about what you are going to do. I am very worried."

"Oh mum, I am still young, I have plenty of time to think about this."

"But what will you do when all your friends start training for jobs or leave Sea Haven for university at the end of the summer holiday?"

"Don't worry mom. I'll think of something."

The telephone rang. Anna was also worried but she did not want to tell her mother this. She went for a walk.

She was a lucky girl who lived in the beautiful town of Sea Haven by the sea and she never wanted to leave it. The town was very busy in the summer as many people came there for a holiday at the seaside. Anna walked on the path by the busy beach.

"Mummy! Mummy!"

A little girl was crying. She was about three years and was alone in the street.

"Are you lost little one?"

"Yes. Mummy gone."

Anna put her arm around her and dried her tears with a handkerchief.

"Let's see if we can find her. Where did you lose her?"

The little girl pointed towards the hotels then the other way towards the sea. A lady suddenly came.

"Lucy! Mummy's here! Where have you been?"

The lady thanked Anna and took Lucy away. Lucy smiled and waved at Anna.

"Could you please help me miss?

A nurse, a volunteer nurse who helped people who got ill on the beach was standing behind her with a man who was just wearing swimming trunks. His skin had many red marks on it especially on his chest.

"Please help me take him to the treatment room."

Anna helped the man walk towards the caravan which had a big red cross on it.

"Jelly fish stung me all over my body. It is very painful."

The man seemed to be in great pain. Anna watched as the nurse put lotion on the stings. The man began to look happier.

Anna left the caravan but bumped into a teenage girl outside. The girl was holding a handkerchief to her nose. There was blood on it.

"Nose bleed?"

The girl nodded in reply to Anna's question.

Anna made the girl sit down on the wall.

"Put your head between your legs. It will stop the bleeding."

After a few minutes, the bleeding had stopped.

Anna helped the girl wash in the Red Cross caravan before leaving.

****

She walked home and into the kitchen.

"Did you have a nice walk, Anna?"

"Yes mum and now I know what I want to do."

"That was a quick decision."

"I knew all the time but had not thought about it. You see, I like to care for people so I think I want to be a nurse."

Mum sat down and hugged her,

"That's a very good idea. You can train at the local hospital and stay in Sea Haven."

Question

A <u>vocation</u> or 'calling' is the type of job which some people feel they must do even if it is hard or low-paid. Why is the profession of nursing seen as a vocation?

Vocabulary

Caravan (n) - a little house on wheels used as temporary accommodation

Handkerchief n) - small fine piece of cloth used to dry eyes, blow nose etc

Jelly fish (n) - live in the sea and sting causing pain and sometimes illness if disturbed

Lotion (n) - liquid put on the body for medical or beauty treatment. Many different kinds of lotion

Vocation (n) - special type of job which includes unselfish service to other people

Volunteer nurse (n) - unpaid nurse who gives basic treatment to minor maladies.

The Wood People

"Heh! Look Phil! Isn't that the new boy Joe walking towards the woods over there?"

"I think you are right Jay. He came to the school a few weeks ago. What is he doing here?

"He could ask us the same question."

"Come on, let's cycle back now before it gets dark. My mum does not like me cycling on the road in the dark."

They watched the boy.

"He's good at football."

"Yes, I know. Very good. In fact he's very good at everything, isn't he? He knows more about maths and science than the teachers and even knows different languages. He talks to Carlos in Spanish and Kim in Korean and everyone wants to be his friend. Like a superman. That's why I think he's strange. No-one is that good at everything."

"So he's clever, talented and popular. Some lucky people are. It doesn't mean he's strange Jay?"

"Yep! You're right. Forget it. It's just people are never that perfect usually. That's all."

"He's gone into the wood now Jay. Let's follow him."

"Good idea. But hurry or we'll lose him."

They hid their bicycles in a bush and took the path into the wood. Ahead, they could just about see Joe's blond head. They did not talk as they did not want Joe to notice them so they walked quietly too. If he looked back he would see them so they tried to run fast between trees as they followed him as though they were spies in a film.

Joe was walking deep into the forest. The boys felt excited as they followed the new boy but also nervous as it was getting dark. It would be difficult to find their way out of the wood.

"Where is he going Phil? We have been walking for half an hour. This is really strange."

"I don't know but I don't want to go home until we find out what's he's doing."

After another twenty minutes Joe turned left. The boys could smell smoke. They hid behind a tree and watched Joe. He was in a clearing and talking to some people who were standing by a fire. The people all looked different. Some were pale skinned, some dark skinned, some tall, some short, some old, some very young .There were some huts and around the edge of the clearing, a garden but it looked as if they were growing vegetables in it, not flowers. They seemed to be living in the forest.

"This is really weird. I don't like it. Let's go home."

"No Phil. They're just camping. Let's go and say hi."

Before Phil could answer Jay walked into the clearing.

"Hi Joe! Are you camping out tonight? Phil and I are lost."

Joe smiled but the other people just stared and came closer.

"That's ok Jay. I can take you back to the forest edge and show you where you left your bicycles. I knew you were following me boys."

"How did you know?"

"We know these things."

 The other people watched and then nodded their heads.

"Come on, it's this way and don't look back'

They followed Joe.

"Are you camping Joe?"

He did not answer. Jay looked back and saw the strangest thing ever.

The people in the clearing were stepping into the fire.

Jay screamed but they did not burn. They simply melted into the flames.

"Phil! Look!"

"Joe. Who are you? Where are you from?'"

"You won't see us again so don't try to find us."

'Who are you?"

But Joe had gone.

Our bikes were still in the bush. Neither of us spoke. What we had seen was like a dream.

We did not even look at each other but cycled home fast.

Question

Why did Jay think Joe was strange?

Vocabulary

Bush (n)-large plant, a shrub

Camping (n) - sleeping and living in a tent or under a basic cover

Spies (n/pl.) - secret agents like 007, James Bond

Strange (adj.) - unusual, not as normal

Weird (adj.) very strange

Close to you

Like millions of other people in London, Holly took the underground train to work every day. She got on the train at exactly 8.10am and she arrived at Kings Cross station at 8.25am. She worked in the city as a secretary and from the tube (underground train) station it was a short walk to her office.

She did not like travelling on the train as it was very crowded, often too hot and boring. Sometimes the train came late or there were so many people that she could not get on the train and had to wait for the next one. A lot of people read a magazine or book on the train. Few people talked. Holly decided that she would do this too. It would make the journey seem faster Although, sometimes she met colleagues from her office Sue, Anne or Cheryl, Barry, Ken or Clive and then they could chat but even that was difficult with so many strangers close who listened.

On the way home, there were free newspapers being given out near the tube station or even on the train which people read then left their copy on the train. The news was mostly about London. There were photographs of pop singers or stories about crimes or new laws or even news about the underground train system. At the back of the free newspaper was a page of messages from people; friends sending messages to friends or strangers to strangers. Some messages were wishing a friend happy birthday but some were more romantic.

Messages

Tall, dark guy would like to get to know pretty girl with red hair wearing a blue top on the* Northern Line going south yesterday at 8am. Want to meet for lunch? Tel.-----
Love at first sight for sweet black-haired girl wearing a red suit with cat brooch and white shirt on *Northern Line to Kings Cross every morning at about 8.15am. Want to meet besotted shy boy? Tel. ------------

*Main train line that between North and South London

Holly re-read the second message and thought about her clothes the day before. She had worn clothes like that yesterday but it was the cat brooch that made her think that she was possibly the one the 'shy boy had loved at first sight."

It was exciting but she did not know who her admirer was. She tried to remember the faces of the people on the train yesterday but could not because she had spent the journey talking to Sue, Ken, Barry and Clive.

The next morning, she got onto the train at the usual place and looked carefully around the train. There were many young men on the train including Barry, Ken and Clive to whom she chatted and forgot to look for possible 'shy boys."

That evening at the back of the newspaper there was another message for her.

Shy boy would like to hear from lovely girl in green and black checked coat and lime green beret asap. Tel. 2223786

That was definitely her and he wanted her to phone a.s.a.p, as soon as possible. At least her journeys to work were more interesting now. Of course she would not telephone until she had some idea who her secret admirer was as he might not be a nice person.

She sent a message which was printed in the next day's free newspaper.

Shy boy- who are you?

His answer was in the next newspaper

Shy boy is tall, dark and handsome with a gsoh like you.

"G.s.o.h.' meant a 'good sense of humour." How did he know that about her?

The following morning she was determined to find her admirer. She slowly looked around the train. She knew many of the faces but few were handsome and the handsome ones were often not tall or were too old to be 'boys.' It was hopeless.

"You look worried Holly.'

It was her office colleague Barry. He, Ken and Sue had got on at the last station. He was standing next to her.

"Not worried exactly Barry just--------."

She looked at Barry again. He was tall with dark hair and good-looking and he even had a good sense of humour. He was the only possible 'shy boy' she could see on the train at the moment.

"Yes. It's me. I hoped you might guess sooner."

"Sorry Barry. It was too obvious I suppose."

They chatted all the way to Kings Cross and Holly never had a boring train journey again.

The London underground train system, 'the tube' has the longest route length in the world (250 miles) and is the third busiest in Europe (after Paris and Moscow). In 2007 one billion passengers were recorded, about three million daily.

As in any big city, it is often difficult to meet a future partner/husband/wife so the Lonely Hearts section in the free newspapers aims to bring strangers together.

Question

How did the messages in the newspaper make Holly's train journeys more interesting?

Vocabulary

A.s.a.p - an abbreviation for **as soon as possible**

Beret (n) - woollen cloth hat often worn on the side of the head. Associated with French but nowadays worn by women everywhere.

Billion (n)-one thousand million

Stranger (n) - person you don't know

Chat (v) - talk about everyday things

Obvious (adj.) - easy to know

The Highwayman

The highwayman came riding, riding, riding,

The highway man came riding, up to the old inn door.

This is part of a well-known English poem by Alfred Noyes which was published in 1906.

From about 1650-1850, highwaymen in England would hide beside busy roads then stop travellers who were on foot, on horseback or in stage coaches and demand their money and valuable things like jewellery. They held guns so people rarely refused them. These thieves of the road have always had a romantic image and the poem is one example which shows this.

The poem, The Highwayman tells a story set in the eighteenth century. The highwayman and the inn-keeper's beautiful daughter were in love. This is their story.

One night the highwayman visits his lover.

"The king's soldiers are hunting for me but I'll be back to see you tomorrow and nothing will stop me my love. Nothing."

"Be careful. I shall die if anything happens to you."

Tears ran down her face.

Her lover galloped away along the long road which twisted across the moor just as she now twisted a long thick lock of her coal black hair around her finger as she watched him ride away.

She did not know that the horse-groom Tim was nearby, listening behind the gate into the courtyard. He felt angry and very jealous.

Why did the beautiful Bess love this criminal and not him? How he wished she sat at her window in the moonlight waiting for him. He seethed. There was one good, certain way to end their love.

The following morning, at the inn, a king's officer who had fallen asleep drunk, late the previous evening, stumbled into the courtyard and called for his horse.

Tim led the horse to him then spoke to him in a low voice.

"Here?' the soldier asked and looked around amazed.

"You'd better be right boy."

Tim smiled.

"Tonight. You'll get your prize. I promise.

The soldiers searched the moors all day for the highwayman but he managed to stay hidden.

As the moon rose, soldiers came marching along the road and up to the inn. They demanded free beer and pushed Bess about. They tied her to her bed and placed a gun so that if she tried to move the bullet would go into her heart.

The soldiers laughed, kissed and taunted her about the highwayman. Eventually they left her alone in her room. She waited patiently listening for the sound of the hooves of his horse coming towards the inn.

She tried to twist off the rope around her wrists so her hands were wet with sweat and blood. Then she heard the hooves of his horse in the distance. Her heart beat fast. When he was quite close she reached for the trigger on the gun and a bullet entered her heart.

The highwayman turned back and rode away into the black night. But news of Bess's death travelled fast. Mad with grief, he galloped away, back onto the road and headed for the inn. A volley of shots rang out from the waiting soldiers and he fell to the ground and breathed his last breath.

Why did people like highwaymen?

It seems that people thought they were brave and daring. The most famous highwaymen were a Frenchman called Claude Duvall and Dick Turpin.

Claude Duvall was 100% the romantic highwayman. He was handsome, brave, charming and did not hurt people. The most famous story about him was that he stopped a stagecoach and demanded "your money or your life."A lady passenger did not want to seem afraid so she began to play her flageolet. According to the story, the highwayman got out his flageolet and accompanied her. He then asked her to dance with him. They danced as the others in the carriage looked on. Because, he had enjoyed himself, he took less money from her before riding away on his horse.

Women particularly liked highwaymen and many stories circulated about them. Unfortunately for these men, they were usually caught and punished by hanging. Both Claude Duvall and the famous Dick Turpin ended like this.

Question

Why were highwaymen popular?

Vocabulary

Courtyard (n) paved area behind a house, often a square or rectangle

Flageolet (n)-small flute blown at the end

Stagecoach (n) - a carriage pulled by horses

Volley (n) of shots- one shot after another

Accompany (v) - play together with

Circulate (v) - go around

Punish (v) - make someone suffer physically or mentally

Seeth (v) - feel very angry silently

References: http://en.wikipedia.org/wiki/Alfred_Noyes

en.wikipedia.org/wiki/**Claude_Duval**

Angry young man

2009

Peter Brown (not his real name) smiled at the headline in the local newspaper.

ELECTRICAL LIFELINE FOR LOCAL FARMERS

It was he who had worked hard to get this electricity supply for these farmers. He then remembered all the help they had given him years ago and the smile left his face when he remembered the bad way he had returned their kindness

****

1990

Peter had to run away. He owed Quinn the gang boss a lot of money but could not pay him back. Things got worse when he tried to break into a rich man's house to steal a painting and nearly got caught so now the police were after him too. He had nowhere to hide and felt like a hunted animal. At the train station, he looked at the DEPARTURES board. The Wetherby train was about to leave. He ran to platform 8 and got on the train.

DEPARTURES	On-board	Time	Platform
WETHERBY	No restaurant car	19.07	8

'Is this going to Wetherby?"

He asked the red-faced man sitting opposite who stopped reading his newspaper to answer.

"Aye, back to Yorkshire and the sooner the better if you ask me."

Peter had never been to Yorkshire but he had heard of it and it sounded as if it might be a good hiding place for him.

****

Edgar and Ida Taddington had lived their whole lives on Holme Farm deep in the Yorkshire countryside. They had never been further than the village five miles away and never wanted to either. Taddingtons had been farming there for hundreds of years. Unfortunately their father had not been a good farmer and to pay off debts, he had sold a lot of their land sixty years ago but there was still the farm-house, and a little land.

Edgar and Ida just kept a few chickens now, sheep and cows and grew enough vegetables and fruit for their own needs. They hardly ever left the farm as everything they needed was there and they were too poor to do anything but live from day to day. Rare visitors were shocked when they came to the farm.

"What no electricity? No water supply? No television? How do you manage?

"We have wood, oil lamps and we have got a well. Taddingtons have been drawing water from that well for years and years so why should we be different?"

They had lived quietly like this all their lives. Their daily work changed with the seasons but one year was like the one before and the one before that until the day they found the boy asleep in the barn.

"Look at the lad Ida. He looks half frozen to death. So thin and pale. Is he still alive?'

The boy woke up and stared into the old man's face.

"Don't be scared lad. Look. You can't sleep out here in this cold weather. Come into the house. Ida will give you some warm milk and you can sleep by the fire.'

Peter was scared and did not know whether he could trust this old man and woman but he was very tired and weak from hunger. Did he really have a choice?

****

He woke up next morning in a feather bed with clean white sheets. He could smell food.

"Eggs, fresh from our chickens and toast. Hungry?

Peter ate and ate. The old couple sat and watched. They had not talked to a young person for a long time.

"What brings you here?

Peter looked at Ida and Edgar. Their faces looked red in the glow of the open fire.

Maybe they had heard about him running away from the police but maybe not.

"Looking for work, aren't I. I got tired after walking so far. That's why I went into your barn.

"Farm work? You can help us here if you want but we can only give you a bed and food."

Peter did not know what to say. He was running away but he had no plan. This farm might be the perfect hiding place for him until the police forgot about him but could he trust these two? They looked nice but Peter knew that bad people could seem nice too when they wanted something. He would have to take a chance.

"Great. Thanks! Can I have some more toast?'

****

Weeks passed. Peter got used to getting water from a well, having food cooked on an open fire and sitting in dark rooms lit by oil lamps. It was strange, like being in another world. They did not even seem to use money much but he knew they had some in a teapot on the dresser. That would be useful later. The old couple asked very little about him luckily so he only had to tell a few lies.

He could have gone on like this for a long time but he was a little bored and wanted to see more people of his own age, not just Ida and Edgar and their friend Joe Grimton who looked at him fiercely and was suspicious of him. Ida and Edgar were quiet but kind. He had never met people like them before so did not understand them.

He wanted to leave but did not know where to go. One thing was certain. He would need money. It was hard to leave as they were nearly always in the house. The only time they went out was when their friend Joe Grimton took them to the weekly cattle market as many of their old friends would be there. That would be his only chance. He would leave when Grimton took them to town.

He felt sad as he saw his last of Ida and Edgar as they got into Grimton's Land Rover. He did not want to steal their money but he had to. They would understand so he filled his pockets and walked along the rough track to the main road.

However, he did not get very far. For a vehicle was driving towards him fast. It was Grimton.

The Land Rover stopped in front of him and Joe jumped out.

"Going somewhere?'

Joe faced him and stared.

"What's in your pockets lad?"

The pockets of his trousers bulged with the pound notes he had taken from the teapot in the kitchen. Joe went towards him and pulled out the notes.

Just at that moment Ida and Edgar got out of the Land Rover.

"We were coming back to bring you to the market. You've never been, have you?"

"The boy's a thief Ida and takes from his good friends," Joe said angrily.

I did not say anything. How could I?

"I'll call the police."

Joe had his mobile phone in his hand. It was time for Peter to run.

"Easy there Joe. Edgar and I gave him the money. It's his. He needs it to start a new life."

Joe looked angry.

"Are you certain of that Ida? You must not let people like him hurt decent folk like you and Edgar.

"Certain."

She had tears in her eyes. It was the worst moment of his life. It was probably then that he vowed to pay them back for all their kindness to him.

****

Peter drove down the smooth driveway that a few years ago had just been a stony track. He had seen to that as he was worried that taxis and other vehicles could not get to the farmhouse if Ida and Edgar needed help fast. They were waiting by the front door as he got out of his car. He hugged them. Peter was now a successful businessman with many friends in the town but these two old farmers were the best friends he could ever have,

Question

"......... but these two were the best friends he could ever have.......

Why does Peter think this?

Vocabulary

Aye- This is the way, Yorkshire people say 'yes'

Cattle (n)-cows

Gang (n) - group of criminals

Headline (n) - Large title on front page of a newspaper

Land Rover (n) - type of 4-wheel drive vehicle

Together forever

"Where are we going Rex? Shouldn't you be working this afternoon?"

"It's a surprise Wanda. It's such beautiful weather Just get into the car honey."

He looked across at his wife-to-be and tried to smile. She smiled back and he felt bad. It was crazy. He could not feel sorry for her now. It was too late.

"Why did you ask me to meet you at this bus-stop on this quiet road Rex?"

"My, oh my, honey, you do have a lot of questions! I was coming down from Ferris Town, sweet one, and I thought it would save time if I met you here. Did you keep it our little secret like I asked Wanda? I don't want my parents to know that I skipped work for a date with you."

"Of course I did Rex. Why do you ask?"

She paused and looked.

"Rex, I have..."

"No reason honey and no more questions. We're here."

Wanda looked at the trees ahead through which she could see the lake. She had visited the huge Blue Crystal Lake before but not this remote part of it. They were in the middle of nowhere with not one person around. She got out of the car.

"Now close your eyes Wanda, hold my hand and follow me."

He led her through the woods. He helped her when she fell over tree roots. She kept her eyes closed and trusted him completely. It was so easy. Soon he would be free.

"Now open them."

Wanda looked at the lake and the wooden rowing boat at the water's edge.

"Look at the water Wanda. It's a lovely afternoon. Perfect for a romantic row on the lake. Don't you agree?"

"Rex. There's something...."

"No more questions, sweet one. Just get in and I will take you wherever your heart desires."

It was useless to say no so Wanda got in. Rex was good at rowing and soon got a long distance from the lakeshore. He looked at Wanda. She was pretty but she was not beautiful like his Elsa who would soon be his wife. If his parents had not made him woo Wanda and more or less force them to get married, he would not have to hurt Wanda. But he had no choice. He had to have Elsa.

He rowed out towards the island as he had planned. Wanda would go overboard into the water. Wanda could not swim and would get caught in the weeds and then she would disappear forever.

She just looked surprised when he took her hand and pulled off her love knot ring (so that she would not be identified if found) and pushed her over the side of the boat and even more surprised when he held her head down under the water. She tried to hold onto the boat and nearly capsized it but in a short time, she was still and disappeared into the water. Crystal Lake was the deepest in the * *state. He looked at the gold love knot ring. His parents had told him to get it for Wanda. When he gave it to her, she had looked at him with her large brown eyes and said.

"See how the white and yellow gold entwine Rex. That's like me and you Rex, 'together for ever."

He felt very calm rowing back to shore. No-one would ever find her body and after a while in the water, no-one would recognise her anyway. He was safe and would escape the punishment for murder in this state which was death.

He hoped he had not got too red in the sun as he had his normal 3pm business appointment with Mr Vance. The whole 'date' with Wanda had only taken up thirty minutes of his time.

He tied the boat to a tree with a rope at the shore and ran through the woods towards the road where his car was parked. His heart stopped. There was a blue Ford parked a few yards from his own. He stared at it and jumped when he heard the voice behind him.

"Heh buddy! Where's Wanda?"

He turned around fast. There was a tall blonde guy behind him.

"Who are you?"

"Didn't she tell you about us? Gee, I was hoping. But wait a minute, I followed you here and watched you take her to the lake so where is she? I.."

The blonde man stopped and stared at Rex's hand. Rex looked at his hand. He still had the love knot ring on his pinkie.

The blonde man's eyes looked strange and he tore at his hair as he came towards Rex.

"What have you done with my Wanda? Where is she? Where is she? Tell me."

Rex's finger must have got fatter and the ring was stuck fast. He could not get it off. He thought of the **electric chair in the State Penitentiary. "Together forever" Wanda had said. But when she said it, she had wanted to be together in life not death, he guessed.

**In some states in the USA, death in an electric chair is the punishment for murder. This story is set in the 1950s.*

Question

Why does Rex think he has no choice but to murder Wanda?

What do you think Wanda was trying to tell Rex?

Vocabulary

Lake (n) - inland area of water

Rowing boat- small boat, moved by oars in the water

Pause (n) - a short silence in a conversation

Pinky (n) – American slang for a person's little finger

Punishment (n) - loss or pain inflicted

Recognise (n) - remember a person from before

Entwine (v)-to twist around another

Skipped work (v) - leave work without permission

Trust (v) - to believe in reliability of a person

Woo (v) - Old-fashioned word which means to behave in a way to make the one you love romantically, love you in return

Calm (adj.) - peaceful

Surprised (adj.) - the reaction to an unexpected thing

Strange (adj.) - unusual.

I get the picture

Tommy Atkins wiped the sweat from his face, swatted a mosquito and took his precious Kodak Brownie camera from the cupboard in his army barracks. Mum and dad had given the camera to him on his last birthday before he was sent out to Malaya from England.

He was free for a few hours that afternoon and would take a few photographs of the barracks. Then he could finish the camera film, get it developed and send the photographs home to mum and dad in England. They had heard of Malaya and knew that it was hot and was covered with a lot of jungle but it would be nice for them to see where their only son was living. It might even make them worry less about him when they could see how modern the barracks were and pretty pictures of Kota Bharu.

The other soldiers were going for lunch and a beer in the town but he preferred taking photographs. He liked photography and was saving up to buy a better camera. He took two photographs of some friends at the air base then cycled down to the beach, Pantai Kuala Pak Amat as it was called by the Malayans. The tide was out and there were few people about as it was very hot under the midday sun. There was just himself and another man nearby. The man was looking out to sea with binoculars and then Tommy saw him focus his camera and take a photo of the beach.

https://uk.images.search.yahoo.com/images/view;_ download.com

Tommy waved. It was Taki from the camera shop. He often talked to Taki about photography and had learnt a lot from him. He spoke very good English which was unusual for a Malayan. He could speak the local Kelantese dialect and his own Chinese language too, Tommy supposed. Taki always seemed to be around the town with his camera just like himself. He had seen him at different places by the coast and even near the air base but that is what it was like when you had a strong interest in something.

Tommy thought that he was lucky to have someone else to chat to about his hobby. His friends in the barracks were not interested in photography at all.

Later that afternoon, he went to Taki's camera shop.

"Good afternoon Mr Tommy. No work today?"

'Yes. I'm free until tomorrow."

Lucky person. When do you soldiers get long holiday Mr Tommy?

"It depends. Only a few get holiday at the same time so the base is always operational. Do you understand?'

"I see. I see. And how many do you need to make it operational? "

"Quite a few Taki! Quite a few. You never know what might happen. I mean what if the Japanese suddenly invaded?

Taki laughed loudly.

"Japanese invade! Very funny Mr Tommy. Very funny." Taki laughed a lot about this idea.

And you Mr Tommy, when do you go home to England? Maybe for your Christmas festival? It maybe soon. Am I right?

"Yes, less than three weeks but I can't go home. Oh no, Taki. England's too far, worst luck. I couldn't even sail back in time for the 25th. That's why I want to get my pictures developed so I can send them by post to my parents.'

Taki took Tommy's camera and took it into the dark room to remove the roll of film.

He returned with Tommy's precious camera and looked so sad that Tommy thought there must be a problem with it.

"Have you ever been to Singapore Tommy? That is good place for holiday. There are many beautiful girls to take pictures of."

"Good idea but I have no long holiday until January."

Taki put his hand on his shoulder and stood with him at the closed door.

"Tommy. It is better in Singapore. Go very soon. This town is not .... It would be good to get away. I must go now.'

Tommy frowned. Taki was being so strange. It worried him.

He said goodbye and left. When he looked in the shop window Taki had already disappeared into the back of the shop.

Tommy thought about his friend Taki's words many times in the next few weeks. It was not until early December that his meaning became clear to Tommy.

There were many rumours about the Japanese in the camp.

"The Japanese are coming. They have been seen in the South China Sea.'

"No. Who told you? It's just scaremongering."

No-one knew what to believe as there were many rumours in wartime until everyone heard the air planes overhead in the early hours of the 8th December.

"The Japanese are landing. There are thousands of them!" Someone ran into the barracks shouting.

Tommy felt very scared and suddenly thought about Taki. He remembered seeing Taki along the beach taking pictures, by the base and even around the town. Taki had tried to warn him. How could he have been such a fool?

"Do you know the Chinese man Taki who has the photography shop?" Tommy asked an air-man who was running past.

"What? Why do you ask such stupid questions at a time like this? We're under attack man and the only camera shop around here belongs to a Japanese man anyway."

Taki was a Japanese. It was all clear to him now but just too late.

Japanese Intelligence Services

Before World War Two, it is claimed that Japanese emigrants to other countries and their descendants were still considered "doha.' "Doha' means Japanese and loyal to the Emperor. In South East Asia including Malaya, many Japanese immigrants worked as barbers, prostitutes, journalists and photographers who allegedly passed on useful information and photographs to the Japanese secret services. In Malaya, there was even a newspaper editor who tried to promote pro- Japan opinion.

In this story, Taki (not his real name) is based on a camera shop owner who sent important information and photographs which helped the Japanese plan their landing and invasion of Malaya at Khota Bahru in northeast Malaya in the early hours of the 8th December 1941.

1.   *Reference:* Journal of Contemporary History - Sage
   www.uk.sagepub.com/lippmanccl2e/study/articles/EverestPhillips.pdf

Question

How would you describe Tommy Atkins?

Vocabulary

I get the picture- expression meaning that you now understand a situation

Attack (under)- being attacked.

Barracks (n) - soldiers living area

Base (air) - Special area for airmen to work in

Beer (n) - alcohol

Dark room (n) - at this time camera film was made into photographs in an unlit room

Emigrant (n) - a person who leaves his country to live in another country.

Immigrant (n)-a person from another country who comes to live in your country

Mosquito (n) - small flying insect that sucks mammal's blood.

Rumour (n) - story which may be true or untrue

Scaremonger (n) – (colloquial) one who makes other people feel worried or scared.

Focus (v) - look closely at something or someone

Invade (v) - go into another's place/area/land

Warn (v) - bring a danger to someone's attention

Operational (adj.) - currently working

The Northern and Southern Lights

www.dailymail.co.uk

Look at the beautiful green light. You can see bright colourful *skies aurora borealis (northern) and aurora australis (southern)* especially at night near the poles,that is the Artic or Antartic. You can see them all the year round but the period of the equinox is the best time (March 20th, June 21st, September 22nd,December 21st).

What causes the polar lights? Simply, gas from the sun travels and is attracted to the Earth's magnetic field which results in charged particles which moves towards the earth's poles. When they meet oxygen and nitrogen atoms, wonderful colourful lights are the result.

The display of lights may be as far as 620 miles away. The colour of the lights is a sign of their distance from the earth.

Ruby Reds	- 240 + kilometres away
Bright green	– between 100-240 kilometres away
Blue violet/reds- Below 100 kilometres away	

Reference-en.wikipedia.org/wiki/**Aurora**_(astronomy)

The Beast on the Moor

For a long time in Britain, many people have been saying that they have seen large cat-like animals in some country areas, particularly on Bodmin moor in Cornwall.. Sheep have been found dead there although scientists say it may be common animals killing the sheep. Some people think there are one or more wild animals like panthers on the moor which used to be someone's illegal pet(s). The mystery continues.

The Brook's family's house was on the same street as the man who was found dead on the moor the night before.

Police detective Ampton stared at Roy Brooks who looked pale and scared.

"I am sorry detective but Brandon Jones and I had been friends since our schooldays so naturally it's a terrible shock."

"Poor Brandon. This terrible animal has got to be caught before he kills anybody else."

Roy Brook's wife Elsie was crying as she said this.

"Why do you say animal Mrs Brooks.?"

"Well, everybody knows, don't they? It's the beast. Everyone knows there's some big, wild animal out on the moor. The farmer's sheep have been killed by it and the dogs. It's terrible. None of us is safe."

"Mrs Brooks. It is only a possibility that the beast killed Brandon. We police will think about this."

The people in the villages near the moor often talked about the very big, strong animal which looked something like a cat and which they said sometimes killed sheep. This was the first time that a human had been found dead with bite marks.

Just then the door bell rang and a woman ran into the room.

Elsie Brooks stood up and put her arms around the woman.

"Clare. It's too awful. Poor, poor Brandon. Come sit down."

The dead man's wife, a tall blonde woman sat next to Elsie on the sofa and started to cry.

"I often warned him not to go jogging on the moor at night but he would not listen to me.'

Police detective Ampton watched the two women.

"So Mrs Jones, did your husband often jog on the moor?"

"Yes detective. Nearly every day."

"And at what time did he usually do this?

"Between 9pm and 11pm usually.'

Ampton looked thoughtful. Mrs Jones had only told the police that her husband was missing at 4am He wondered why she had waited such a long time before calling the police.

He had a telephone call. It was the doctor. As he left the Brook's house he saw a chewed up looking ball in the kitchen. The Brooks had no children and there was no dog in the house. He picked up the red rubber ball which was covered with teeth marks. Mrs Brooks seemed to read his thoughts

"It was Trixie's and Rolf's ball. They were our guard dogs but they disappeared three days ago. I used to take them for walks on the moor in the evening. The beast must have followed us home because when I went out into the garden to give them their meat three days ago, they were gone. It's just too much! First, my two lovely dogs and now Brandon!"

Elsie Brooks started to cry loudly.

Ampton thought that Mrs Brooks must be an emotional woman especially crying so much about guard dogs and her husband's friend..

A young policeman came and gave him a piece of paper.

"This was found near the dead man's body sir.'

It was a torn piece of paper

Meet   1

Br

Lo

x

"This is lucky PC Davis. You see the murdered man had received a note about meeting someone. I wonder who sent it ?"

Ampton walked away from the houses and towards the moor. He wanted to go and see where Brandon Jones had last been alive. The weather was cold and the wind blew strongly across the moor. It was a strange place to meet someone unless it was a secret meeting for few people would be walking on the moor in this weather at night. Ampton looked at the note again.

Meet 1

Br

Lo

x

The **1 in** the note must refer to a time, either 1, 10, 11, 12 and either am or pm and the **Lo**, very possibly love but maybe not. However, if it was love, the fateful meeting for Brandon must have been a romantic one and not with his wife probably. He could have met a lover before being meeting the beast or his killer as it was true, deep cuts to the face did look as if an animal had attacked the unlucky man.

There were many police officers where Brandon's body had been found. PC Drew came to him.

"Not sure if there's a connection sir but …"

"You have found two dead dogs."

PC Drew looked surprised.

"Very clever sir! Yes, two Rottweiler dogs, ugly animals but how did you know?

"One of the victim's neighbours and friends has lost her dogs. Do you think the beast killed the dogs, PC Drew?"

"I don't think so sir. Forensics say that at first it looked as if they had been savaged by another animal but when they looked more closely, the marks were more like deep cuts from an axe not an animal's teeth marks.

'An axe you say?"

****

Ampton next called on the dead man's wife Mrs Jones. She was outside the house when he called carrying a basket of logs towards the front door.

"A good log fire is wonderful on such a cold day Mrs Jones.'

She smiled.

'It's apple tree wood. It is a bit damp but gives out a lot of heat after a while.'

He followed her into the house.

'How well do you know the Brooks family?'

'Peter is, sorry, I mean was a great friend of Brandon's from school and naturally, we used to have dinner or drinks together sometimes.'

'Would you say you were close?"

Mrs Jones looked thoughtful.

'Yes the Brooks were very close to him, I mean, us. Very close.

"Tell me Mrs Jones, why did you wait so long before calling the police?"

"I thought he may have met some friends and gone for a drink with them. He sometimes did that and would then return home late."

"Really. Who?"

Mrs Jones looked surprised.

"I'm afraid I don't know detective. Brandon had a lot of friends."

The detective left Mrs Jones staring at the fire. He let himself out but walked up the side of the house and smiled when he saw exactly what he had expected to find there.

****

Ampton walked into the police station with a long thin object under his arm. He showed it to PC Davis.

"Could the marks on the dogs have come from this axe-head?"

PC Davis looked at the axe-head carefully.

'Yes sir.'

"I think we have our murderer then."

He gathered the investigation team together.

I found this axe in Jones's garden near a pile of logs that Mrs Jones had chopped for her fire.

'You mean Mrs Jones killed her friends' dogs. Why?"

Ampton was quiet before he began to explain.

'Mrs Brooks was much more upset than either her husband or Mrs Jones about Brandon's death and she used to walk the dogs on the moor late at night when Brandon went for his usual jog.'

'So the two were lovers, you suggest.'

'Yes and Mrs Jones found out. Naturally, she was angry and the stories about the beast on the moor gave her the idea of killing Brandon. But she had the problem of making it look as if he'd been attacked by the beast on the moor.'

'Ah, so you think she stole the dogs and set them on her husband Brandon.'

'Exactly and then after they had killed Brandon she took them to another part of the moor and tried to make it look as if they had been killed by the beast too.'

****

Mrs Jones said nothing to Ampton when she opened the door to her house. He followed her to the sitting room.

"Please tell me the truth Mrs Jones."

Mrs Jones looked into the apple wood fire before answering.

I kept the dogs in an old, empty cottage on the moor and didn't feed them to make them very hungry. Rottweilers are strong and aggressive like the beast. It seemed like the perfect plan then, especially as it meant that stupid, hateful Elsie Brooks would lose the things she loved best: the dogs and my bad husband Brandon.'

'Not quite perfect enough Mrs Jones.'

'How did you know it was me?'

'Very simple. You did not seem at all sad about your husband's death unlike Mrs Brooks. This was the first and most important clue.'

"So is there a beast Detective Ampton?"

Ampton looked hard at her and thought about all the other two-legged beasts he had met in his life. "I don't know Mrs Jones but I'm afraid I must arrest you and take you to the station now so that we can have the full story."

Question

'Very simple. You did not seem at all sad about your husband's death unlike Mrs Brooks. This was the first and most important clue.'

What were the other 3 important clues that helped Ampton solve this case?

Vocabulary

Detective (n) - Higher level policeman who tries to solve crimes

Marks on the body (n) - changes to normal appearance

Moor (n)-large area of unfarmed land

Panther (n)-leopard with black fur

Secret (n)-information known to one or small number of people.

Shock (n) - a big surprise. Often unpleasant.

Arrest (v)-forcefully stop and take a crime suspect to the police station

Disappear (v) - go out of sight

Kill (v) - end the life of a living thing

Walk (a dog) (v) - exercise a dog usually while they are on a lead/leash

Aggressive (adj.) - attacking mood

Dead (adj.) - not alive

Illegal (adj.) - against the law

Lucky (adj.) - unseen powers favour you

Murdered (adj.) - killed with intention

Perfect (adj.)-100% good for you

Strong (adj.) - has great force or power

Terrible (adj.)- very bad

Torn (adj.)-pulled apart

Wild (adj.)- not trained or controlled.

Wonderful (adj.) - Very good

Answers to the questions

The lost dog

She did not feel so sad because she had the girl as well as the dog as friends.

Paradise Hotel

Everything seems perfect to Val in this place eg. the beautiful house and gardens.

The brave villagers of Eyam

He was bitten by a flea that was in the cloth he had received from London. The flea was a carrier of the bubonic plague

Symptoms (in order)

Headache and sick feeling

Fever

Red spots

Black spots

Great pain

Lady Godiva

He did not want to reduce taxes so he gave Godiva, his wife, a challenge which he thought she would not dare to take up.

Horse Shoe Crabs

1. They are ground up and used as fertiliser.
2. They are used a fisherman's bait for eels.
3. Their blood contains *limulus amebocyte* which clots when in contact with bacterial endotoxins (harmful to humans) so their blood is used to detect the presence of dangerous endotoxins.

Double Act

Word	Definition
Engagement(n)	An event which you have agreed or planned to attend previously.
Signature(n)	Usually handwritten signing of a name
Perfect(adj)	100% good in your opinion
Network(v)	Make contact with people for business
Impersonate(v)	Pretend to be someone else
Chit chat(n)	Talk about every day things
Socialise(v)	Chat and mix with other people

The strange story of Madeleine Smith

This case is famous as it made legal history. It had the first 'not proven' verdict in Scottish legal history.

True Love

Noun	Adjective
Silliness	Silly
Misery	Miserable
Anger	Angry
Happiness	Happy
Arrogance	Arrogant
Foolishness	Foolish
Embarrassment	Embarrassed
Blindness	Blind

A taste of his own medicine

First wrong- The antique dealer Fothergill cheated Auntie Agatha.

Second wrong- Tom misled the antique dealer Fothergill by asking for and getting 1200 pounds for the cat when it was worth much less.

Hallowe'en

The Celts believed that their ancestors left the world of the dead *Sannhain* on this day so they welcomed them and lit their way with lanterns.

Words that wound

1. Various possible answers.

Eg. Yes, it makes them think about the damage their hard words cause.

Eg. No, it damages a good chair and does not help a person become more sef-controlled.

2. Various possible answers.

Eg. Telling lies and the story of *'The boy who called wolf"*, one of Aesop's *fables.*

Baby Sherman

Possible answers-

Sherman obeys him

Sherman laughs at him

He is Sherman's uncle which makes him feel proud and mature

Sherman found the twenty pounds he had lost.

Time goes fast when he is with Sherman

Tell-tale

Lucky- He did not have to murder Mrs Crawford as she died anyway

Unlucky- Mrs Crawford somehow found out about his past and used the information to blackmail him

One good turn deserves another

1. Myra meant that Bill should look after his own family before other people.

2. He lent money to friends eg. Peter and David
He agreed to take Mr Jackson's lorry load to Rotterdam even though he did not really want to go.
He helped an illegal immigrant instead of handing him over to the police.

Stolen Good

Chas burgled the house as he needed money for Christmas

His act of kindness which was a risk for him, was delivering the letter to reunite the two old friends.

Parents Evening

Word	Definition
Talent(n)	A natural ability to do something
Gift(n)	A natural ability to do something
Treasure(n)	An object/thing or collection which is/are special and/or valuable
Precious(adj)	Greatly valued or loved
Corridor(n)	Passage giving access to rooms
Unique(adj)	Only one of its kind. Sometimes used loosely to mean very unusual

Vocation

Looking after people who are ill or dying is hard work, difficult and requires a kind heart.

Close to you

She wanted to see if she could discover the identity of her secret admirer.

The Wood People

Joe was unusually multi-talented ie. Clever at school, sport and well-liked by everyone. This made Jay suspicious.

The Highwayman

For many people especially women, highwaymen were romantic figures who were brave, daring and charming like Claude Duvall, the famous French highwayman.

Angry young man

He thought they were the best friends he could ever have as when he was running away, they helped him without asking any questions and even told lies for him after he had stolen from them. Their lies protected him from being arrested by the police.

Together forever

His parents are forcing him to marry her when he really wants to marry Elsa.

She was trying to tell Rex that she loved another man, the blonde man whom Rex met after the murder.

I get the picture

Possible answers

Tommy seems friendly (to Taki)

Enthusiastic (about photography)

Stupid-he did not realise that Taki was Japanese

Innocent- he was fooled easily by Taki

Northern and southern lights-No question

The beast on the moor

1. Note   2. Dog's ball   3. The axe

May
m

Lapis na kulay

Crng

Made in the USA
San Bernardino, CA
02 August 2019

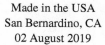

45994838R00051